THE GIFT

Much Love!

Anthony Carnabuci

THE GIFT

by Aliana Brodmann

illustrated by Anthony Carnabuci

ALADDIN PAPERBACKS

First Aladdin Paperbacks edition September 1998

Text copyright © 1993 by Aliana Brodmann
Illustrations copyright © 1993 by Anthony Carnabuci

Aladdin Paperbacks
An imprint of Simon & Schuster
Children's Publishing Division
1230 Avenue of the Americas
New York, NY 10020

Printed and bound in the United States of America

10 9 8 7 6 5 4 3 2 1

The Library of Congress has cataloged the hardcover edition as follows:
Brodmann, Aliana. The gift / by Aliana Brodmann ; illustrated by
Anthony Carnabuci. Summary: In post-World War II Germany, a young girl
visits various shops before deciding how to spend the money
her father has given her for Hanukkah.
[1. Hanukkah—Fiction.   2. Germany—Fiction.   3. Shopping—Fiction.]
I. Carnabuci, Anthony, ill.   II. Title.
PZ7.B78612Gi   1993   [E]—dc20   CIP   92-7887
ISBN 0-671-75110-7
ISBN 0-689-82240-5 (Aladdin pbk.)

For Prof. Dr. Theodor Brüggemann, my patient teacher, mentor, and friend,
whose encouragement sustained me through the years,
in gratitude and with much love — AB

To my father, mother, and brothers,
whose support and love made this book possible — AC

I remember the first year Father gave me a five-mark piece for Hanukkah. In those days in Germany, that was a lot of money. I thought I could buy the whole world if I wanted. That night I fell asleep with the five-mark piece in my hand, barely able to close my fingers around the large, round coin.

The next day at school I kept reaching into my pocket to make sure the coin was still there. I could hardly pay attention because my head was full of ideas about how to spend the money.

On my way home I passed by all my favorite shops. First I went into the stationery store. I always admired the fountain pens when I came to buy pencils. There were particularly important-looking ones in silk-lined boxes set out in the glass display case. I was sure those were the kind that famous writers used.

When the tall, thin lady behind the counter asked me what I wanted, I pointed to a gold-tipped pen as blue as the winter sky. She took out a small bottle of ink, dipped the pen, and drew the ink up into it. Then she handed the pen to me. I laid my five-mark piece on the counter, put the pen between my fingers, and tried to write on the big white pad. The letters didn't come out quite the way I intended. I tried several other pens, but I couldn't make up my mind. So I took back my money and walked on.

    In the bakery window there was a whole row of
gingerbread men holding little white clay pipes in
front of their bellies. I knew just how sweet and
spicy the gingerbread tasted. And with one of
those clay pipes and a bowl of sudsy water, I could
blow the most wonderful rainbow-colored
bubbles. Undecided, I lingered before the display.

A woman walked into the apothecary next door. I always liked going there with my mother. All four walls were lined with shelves from the floor to the tall ceiling. On them were inumerable boxes and containers packed with soaps, bath salts, creams, and lotions. Because it was Christmastime, the boxes were most beautifully wrapped in colored papers and tied with ropes of silver and gold. Exotic fragrances mingled in the air. The shop owner was a short, round man with a polished bald head and whiskers. He knew me well and always had a miniature perfume bottle or a special little soap for me.

What I liked best were the two-sided mirrors that lay in a basket near the big cash register. One side was a regular mirror, the other was like a magnifying glass. When I held it close to my face, I could see the different colors in the iris of my eye. My irises are brown and green with yellow speckles. When I held the mirror farther away, my face became bigger and fuzzier in it.

The shop owner leaned over the counter and gave me an extra big smile. I held the mirror to his face. His smile covered the whole mirror. Quickly, I put it down again.

Miss Lili, the lady in the hat shop, saw me passing by and waved to me. I walked down the three steps into her store. My mother occasionally had a hat designed by her and often just stopped by to chat. All over the store there were ladies' torsos with hats on their heads. Some of them smiled into space demurely while others seemed to forever ponder something distant, just like Miss Lili.

Miss Lili lifted her newest creation off a stand and showed it to me. It sparkled with sequins and rhinestones. The hat I liked best was made of white felt with a wide brim and a scarf that tied under the chin in an enormous bow. I sat on a chair in front of the big three-way mirror and admired myself in the hat. Miss Lili seemed pleased. She gave me a shiny red apple.

I crossed the main street to get to the toy store.
Its neon sign shone brightly through the wintry
twilight, beckoning me inside. Bells jingled as
I pushed open the heavy door. For a moment
I stood absolutely still. I hardly knew where to
look first. There were rows and rows of dolls in
rectangular boxes, reaching out their arms toward
me. Plush bears growled on command. A wooden
duck with six ducklings on wheels was moving
across the floor in front of me.

On one of the counters there was a collection of windup toys. There was a cat with a drum, ballerina mice in colorful tutus, a bear with cymbals, and monkeys with trumpets and tambourines. One by one I wound them up until they all danced and played together.

Each one cost four marks and fifty pfennigs. I would even have some money left over to buy a little bag of roasted chestnuts at the kiosk on the way home. As I tried to make up my mind, the windup toys began to slow down and the monkeys' tambourines gave their last tiny jingles.

"Well?" asked the saleslady, who had approached me.

I reached for the five-mark piece in my pocket. There it was, big and round in my hand. I held on to it and left the store quickly.

It was getting dark outside. Soft white snowflakes were drifting in the air. People seemed to be walking more briskly. But I stopped in front of the pet store. How I wished for a puppy or a kitten. I would even settle for a hamster or a mouse. There was a basket of tiny gray kittens in the display window. One of them had four white paws.

I was thinking about names for the kittens when I heard a beautiful tune. It came from an accordion player who was sitting among a pile of blankets in front of the grocery market.

People passed him by, some of them carelessly dropping a groschen into the hat beside him.

I don't know how long I stood in front of the musician, listening to his lovely music. The stores around were closing up one by one. I could hear the clanging of keys being turned in door locks. Metal shutters rattled against display windows and fell into place. People were rushing by to get home with their packages. Only the musician's tune continued soft and slow through the busy evening.

I slid my hand into my pocket and touched the five-mark piece. Quickly, I tossed it into the hat. He was not supposed to notice, but I think he saw it, anyway.

"Come," he said, "sit by me and I will show you how to play."

Hesitantly, I set down my schoolbag on the sidewalk. It had already gotten rather late. When he placed the accordion on my lap, I was surprised at how heavy it was. He showed me how to pull it apart and push it together slowly. His fingertips pressed against mine on the little buttons that made the sounds.

The winter cold pinched at my nose and cheeks, but I was happy as never before. Soon the musician had taught me enough so that we could play a tune together. It sounded as though we had been practicing for a long time. Another tune followed, and then another. I was almost able to play by myself.

The snow was now blowing harder, but people stopped anyhow to watch and listen. Coins kept dropping into the hat. I knew I had to be home by the time the first star appeared, but I hoped it would be a long while until then and that this wonderful evening would last forever.